THE
SURFIN' SPOON

Sebi Gets Barreled

By Jesse & Whitney Hines

Illustrated by Ben Weiland

"Not to us, Lord, not to us but to Your name be the glory, because of your love and faithfulness." Psalm 115:1

2015 Arctic Spoon Publishing
Edited by Matt Pruett
Pages 34/35 inspired by a photo by Matt Lusk

This is Sebi the Spoon.
Sebi is a surfer.

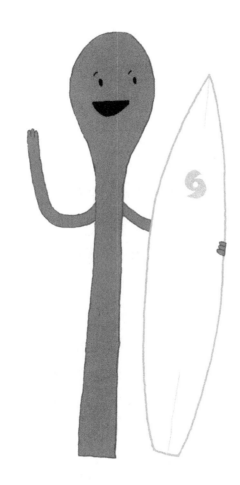

Sebi surfed every day with his BROS, Chicken and Pepé.

YEW!

Chicken and Pepé had grown up surfing, but Sebi
was still learning the tricks they already knew.

More than anything, Sebi wanted to get
BARRELED, which meant riding inside of
a wave. Chicken always got BARRELED
so Sebi asked him for tips.

They were on their way, and the waves were PUMPING.

9

Surfers from everywhere
came to the lighthouse to get
BARRELED; even Scrub, the
toughest spoon in Sebi's school.

You don't have what it takes, GROM.

Although Scrub hurt his feelings, Sebi paddled out. He was nervous.

A GNARLY wave came to Sebi. He was scared, but paddled for it anyway.

He AIR DROPPED...

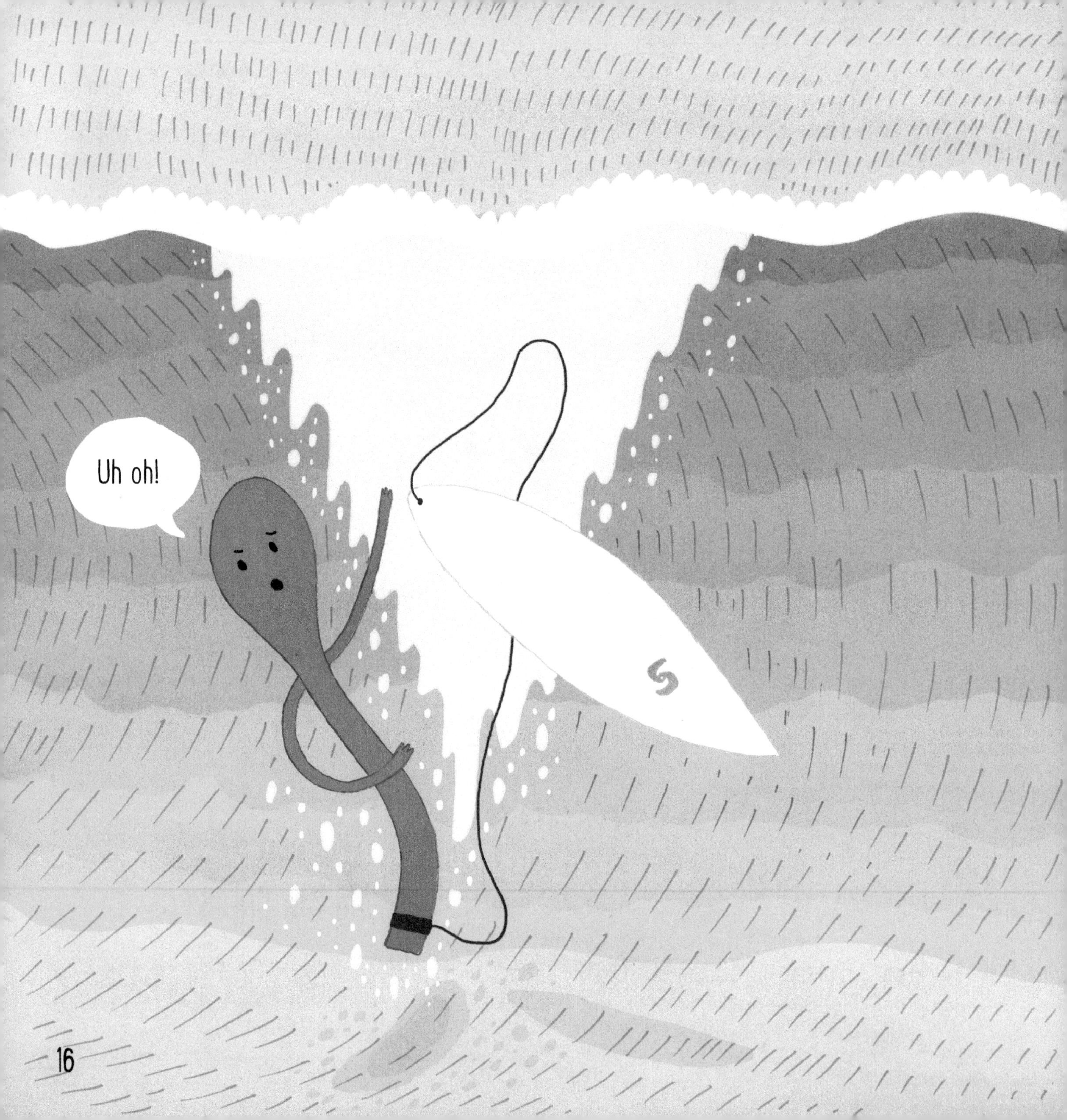
Uh oh!

...and ATE IT.

When Sebi came up, his STICK was BUSTED.

Sebi got to the beach and saw Scrub holding
half of the broken board.

I knew you didn't have
what it takes. Now you
don't even have a board.

As he skated away with his head down...

...Sebi didn't notice a sea turtle on the road in front of him; he BAILED to avoid hitting it!

Sebi broke his elbow. The doctor put his arm in a cast.

No surfing for a while, Sebi.

Chicken and Pepé knew Sebi was BUMMED OUT, so they brought him a new surfboard.

Weeks later, Sebi got his cast off just in time
for another big swell at THE LIGHTHOUSE.

Sebi was STOKED to get another shot at getting BARRELED, but as he went to paddle out, Scrub stopped him.

Remember what happened last time? You ATE IT.

Sebi was about to give up.

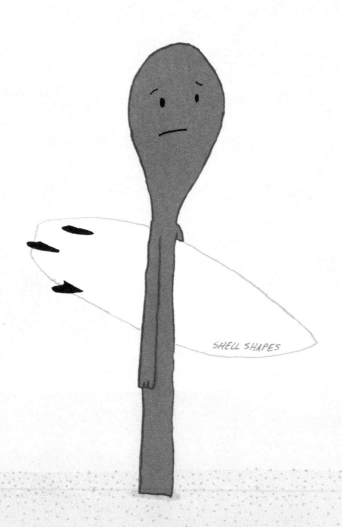

But then Sebi saw Pepé catch an EPIC wave.

If he can do it, so can I!

Sebi quickly made it OUTSIDE and joined
Chicken and Pepé in the LINEUP.

Suddenly, the perfect wave rolled in.
Sebi CHARGED IT. He made THE DROP.

Sebi SET HIS RAIL.

The CURTAIN folded over him...

...Sebi was BARRELED.

Sebi came flying out with the SPIT.
Everyone cheered for Sebi's wave!

Once Sebi had gotten BARRELED,
it was all he could think about.

But more than catching the perfect wave,
Sebi learned an important lesson.

42

Never give up on your dreams,
no matter what gets in the way.

GLOSSARY

(Order of appearance)

BROS – friends
YEWW – a cheer of excitement
BARRELED – riding inside of a wave
THE LIGHTHOUSE – the surf break in front of the Cape Hatteras Lighthouse
PUMPING – really good
GROM – a young kid
GNARLY – strong, challenging
AIR DROPPED – being completely disconnected from the wave
ATE IT – a bad fall or wipeout
STICK – surfboard
BUSTED – broken
BAILED – purposely jumping off

BUMMED OUT – sad

RAD – awesome

STOKED – happy

EPIC – perfect

OUTSIDE – past the breaking waves

LINEUP – where surfers wait for waves

CHARGED IT – completely committed

THE DROP – riding down the wave after catching it

SET HIS RAIL – directing the surfboard to ride the wave

CURTAIN – the curl of the wave

SPIT – when the water inside of the wave forcefully makes its way out

The AUTHORS

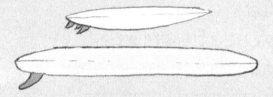

Jesse is a former professional surfer from the Outer Banks. He's been shredding and traveling all over the world since age 14. Whitney is a surfer and artist who creates pottery in her studio, "the mud room." They live with their son, Bear, in Kitty Hawk, North Carolina. In 2012 they opened the Surfin' Spoon Frozen Yogurt Bar.

This book is based on Jesse's life and his surfing adventures.

The ILLUSTRATOR

Ben Weiland is an illustrator, filmmaker and designer who is interested in surf exploration along cold coastlines. He runs a website called Arctic Surf and became friends with Jesse on a surf trip to the South Island of New Zealand. Ben lives in Carlsbad, California.

CPSIA information can be obtained at www.ICGtesting.com
Printed in the USA
LVOW02s2008080815

449085LV00004B/5/P